I Didn't Do It

a story about responsibility

Sarah Read

To Get "The Anxious Monster" for FREE!

THIS BOOK BELONGS TO

....

....

Hi! My name is Sophia, and I love to have fun.
I always enjoy playing outside in the sun.
I like playing with my brother, my mom and my dad.
We have many fun adventures, and that makes me feel glad.

Sometimes accidents happen while I am at play.
For instance, one of my toys broke just the other day.
My brother, Jacob, had wanted to see my favorite doll.
When he picked it up, I said, "That's mine! Go play with your ball."

I grabbed back my doll and gave it a good yank.
When her head popped off, oh, how my heart sank.
"Sophia!" Jacob cried. "Why did you do that?"
"It is not my fault," I argued. "I thought you might use her as a bat."

Then Jacob did something I
didn't know anyone could do.

When he held out his hand, I gave
him the doll's head and body too.

With a twist and a pop, he made
my doll whole in a whirl.

Then he handed her back with a
flourish as he gave her a twirl.

In the morning, Mom called out that it was time for school.

But I couldn't find my homework, which wasn't very cool!

"Mom, my homework is missing. I can't find it in this mess."

Mom looked into my room and pointed. "Is that it poking out from under that dress?"

It was there. But losing it wasn't my fault, that was for sure.
Anyone would have trouble finding things on my messy floor.
"If you clean your room, finding things won't be so hard," Mom said.
Thank goodness she didn't mention the mess under my bed!

During quiet time at school, I sat reading in my chair.
Then I went to talk to my friend. I said, "I love your hair!"
Emily smiled at me and pressed a finger to her lips.
Our teacher came over with her hands on her hips.

"It's reading time, Sophia," Miss Joy whispered quietly.
"Did you have to speak right now? Is it an emergency?"
"No, but it's not my fault. Sometimes I can't control my mouth."
I crossed my eyes to look at my lips down south.

"And who decides what your mouth says?" Miss Joy asked curiously.
"Well, my brain..." I said, then shrugged and flashed a smile easily.
She said, "You must take responsibility when you've done something wrong.
Admitting your behavior helps you improve, and it won't take long!"

On my birthday, Mom made a double-layered chocolate cake.

She let me taste the yummy batter. I couldn't wait for it to bake!

Mom let it cool before she frosted it; it would be a while before we ate.

But my tummy growled, and I wasn't sure how long I could wait.

I tried to be patient as I stared at the tasty treat.

But, I couldn't restrain myself; I took a swipe of frosting to eat.

"Sophia, did you just stick your finger in your cake?" asked Dad.

It's not my fault. It looked too good! I wanted to say really bad.

Instead, I thought of Miss Joy's words about responsibility.
"I'm sorry. I ate some frosting." I practiced my new ability.
When Dad thanked me for admitting it, I felt as light as air.
"We can fix it together," he said. "Why don't you pull up a chair?"

Responsibility is a good skill for everyone to learn.
So, give it a try sometime. Good luck. It is now your turn!

The End

What Did You Think of *I Didn't Do It*?

Thank you for purchasing this book. I know you could have picked any number of books to read, but you picked this book and for that I am extremely grateful.

If you like the book... and if you'd be willing to spare just two or three minutes...would you be willing to share your review of the book on Amazon?

If you would, it would mean the absolute world to me!

Thank you SO much. This helps to get the book into as many hands as possible, helping other parents and educators!

I really appreciate all your support!

Sarah Read
children's book author

Thank you!

To Get "The Anxious Monster" for FREE!

SCAN ME

Made in United States
North Haven, CT
17 June 2023